CHUBBY BUNNY

BY JULIE MURPHY

PICTURES BY SARAH WINIFRED SEARLE

BALZER & BRAY
An Imprint of HarperCollinsPublishers

Barbara "Bunny" Binks came from a long line of Barbaras.

Which is why Bunny went by Bunny, her mother went by Babs, and her grandmother went by, well—Barbara! Grammy Barbara was short and thin with a long nose. Babs was tall and round with big blue eyes. And Bunny was just plain old round with rosy cheeks that made everyone smile.

Bunny loved her nickname. She had a white spotted
bunny named Ralph. And since she didn't have real bunny
ears, she wore her hair in two buns on top of her head.
Her mother called them bunny buns!

"Are you excited for today, Bunny?" her mother asked at breakfast.

"More excited than a rabbit in a carrot patch," Bunny told her. She had been looking forward to this day for weeks. It was finally field day at school!

As she got dressed and her mother did her hair, Bunny told her, "Make my buns extra tight! I need my bunny buns to stay right where they're supposed to be today."

"Two extra-tight bunny buns for my honeybun—coming right up!" her mother said.

At field day, Bunny and her classmates competed in a three-legged race, an egg-balancing obstacle course, and even a wheelbarrow race.

By snack time, Miss Miller's Purple Cows and Mr. Treviño's Laughing Lilies had won the same number of events. Principal Simmons agreed that there was only one way to settle a tie.

Bunny clapped her hands. This was her favorite game. She loved marshmallows!

"I need two volunteers," said Miss Miller.
Bunny's arm shot into the air. So did Parker Pell's.
Miss Miller picked them both.

"On your mark," said Principal Simmons into his bullhorn. "Get set! Eat!"

Bunny shoved a marshmallow into her mouth and so did Parker.

Bunny added marshmallow after marshmallow as her classmates chanted her name.

Parker looked queasy. He tried to say "chubby bunny," but it came out sounding like something else.

"Look at that chubby Bunny shove those marshmallows in her mouth!" cried someone from the crowd.

"No wonder she's winning!"

Suddenly Bunny didn't feel so good, and it wasn't because of the marshmallows.

Bunny looked out to see the whole school laughing and pointing at her.

She spat out the marshmallows and
ran home.

"Hello, my Bunny bun!" Bunny's mother greeted her.
"I made your favorite—a marshmallow, peanut butter,
and banana sandwich!"
"Don't call me that!" Bunny said.
"And I hate marshmallows!"

Bunny ran to her room and pulled her bunny buns down.
She sat with Ralph and cried.

Bunny's mother came to check on her. "What's wrong?"
So Bunny told her the whole sticky story.

"You know what? I think tomorrow everyone will have forgotten all about Chubby Bunny."

Bunny didn't know if that was true, but maybe she could help them forget. . . . First, she would need a plan.

The next day during recess, Bunny sat in a tree with a bag full of marshmallows. Maybe the way to make everyone forget about the incident was to create a distraction.

She waited for Parker to step under the tree.

Bunny jumped.

Miss Miller shrieked.

Uh-oh.

Bunny was in a
sticky situation.

"I'm sorry," Bunny said, and she meant it. She never meant to hit Miss Miller or ruin her pretty hair. "I just wanted people to stop calling me Chubby Bunny."

Maybe she could impress everyone with her brilliance! "According to my very scientific calculations, this marshmallow will turn bright blue when I . . ."

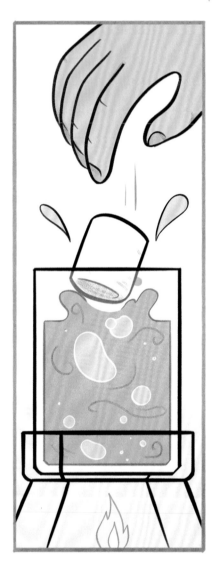
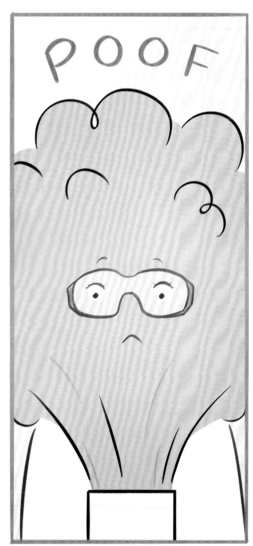

"I guess she's not a Smarty Bunny," said Rebecca Roper

She'd always been able to make people laugh. She could be the class clown!

"Psst!!" Bunny whispered to Dylan Dawkins in a deep voice. "Did you hear that joke Bunny told this morning? We should call her Funny Bunny."

"I didn't hear any joke from Bunny!" Parker said.

That night, Grammy Barbara
came over and brought
Bunny's favorite dessert,
marshmallow pie.
"No thank you," said Bunny.
"I'm allergic to marshmallows."

"What's gotten into my Bunny?
And where are your bunny ears?"
Bunny couldn't keep any
secrets from Grammy Barbara,
so she told her everything.

"Do you think you're chubby?" Grammy Barbara asked.

Bunny looked down. "Yes."

"And why is that a bad thing?"

"Well . . ." Bunny tried to answer, but the only bad thing about being chubby was when other people were mean about it.

Grammy Barbara smiled. "I like the name Chubby Bunny. And I think you're very clever and funny and pretty. And chubby too!"

"Yeah?" Bunny asked.

"Being chubby isn't a bad thing, and maybe you can help other people understand that too. Now, how about some of that pie?"

The next day at school, Bunny marched into school straight and tall.

"Good morning, Chubby Bunny!" said Dylan Dawkins.

"Chubby Bunny!" a few classmates sang in a singsong voice.

Miss Miller put her hands on her hips. "Class, I don't think Bunny likes that nickname."

"Actually," said Bunny, "I don't think there's anything wrong with Chubby Bunny or with being chubby. Or with being tall like Rebecca or wearing glasses like Dylan."

Bunny pulled a bag of marshmallows out of her backpack. "But if you're going to call me Chubby Bunny, you should say it with a marshmallow in your mouth!"

Miss Miller helped Bunny hand out marshmallows to the whole class.

"Okay!" said Bunny as she stood proudly on her chair for the whole class to see. "On the count of three. One, two, three!"